D0131879

Chimp with a limp

Lesley Sims

Illustrated by David Semple

"Hurray!" sings Chimp.
"I'm off to play."

"I'll swing and slide and ride all day."

He nears the gate.
Then he hears, "Wait!"

It's Cheetah
with a heavy crate.

"Can you help me haul this home?
It's hard to heave it on my own."

I caught some pirates stealing gold...

...I fought them. I was feeling bold.

I tripped and slipped
upon the deck.

One slung a hook
around my neck.

*They made me
walk the plank
you see...*

*...and, well,
I fell into
the sea.*

I almost drowned.

Then it went dark.

I found I was inside a shark!

"Ha! Ha! Great joke," croaks Frog.
"Some tale."

"It WAS a shark," says Chimp,
"or whale."

It gave a burp.
I shot out...

I had a hunch I'd be their lunch.

They looked a hungry,
munching bunch.

I ran until I reached my door,

battered, bruised
and oh, so sore.

Frog frowns. "I'm sure you are okay.
I saw you on your way to play."

"You have no limp, Chimp?"
Cheetah growls.

Am I a chump?

Now Cheetah scowls.

About phonics

Phonics is a method of teaching reading used extensively in today's schools. At its heart is an emphasis on identifying the *sounds* of letters, or combinations of letters, that are then put together to make words. These sounds are known as phonemes.

Starting to read
Learning to read is an important milestone for any child. The process can begin well before children start to learn letters and put them together to read words. The sooner children can discover books and enjoy stories and language, the better they will be prepared for reading themselves, first with the help of an adult and then independently.

You can find out more about phonics on the Usborne Very First Reading website, **www.usborne.com/veryfirstreading** (US readers go to **www.veryfirstreading.com**). Click on the **Parents** tab at the top of the page, then scroll down and click on **About synthetic phonics**.

Phonemic awareness

An important early stage in pre-reading and early reading is developing phonemic awareness: that is, listening out for the sounds within words. Rhymes, rhyming stories and alliteration are excellent ways of encouraging phonemic awareness.

In this story, your child will soon identify the *i* sound, as in **chimp** and **limp** or **fixed** or **sings**. Look out, too, for rhymes such as **tripped** – **slipped** and **hunch** – **lunch**.

Hearing your child read

If your child is reading a story to you, don't rush to correct mistakes, but be ready to prompt or guide if he or she is struggling. Above all, do give plenty of praise and encouragement.

Edited by Jenny Tyler
Designed by Hope Reynolds

Reading consultants: Alison Kelly and Anne Washtell

First published in 2017 by Usborne Publishing Ltd., Usborne House, 83-85 Saffron Hill, London EC1N 8RT, England.
www.usborne.com Copyright © 2017 Usborne Publishing Ltd.

All rights reserved. No part of this publication may be reproduced, stored in a retrieval system or transmitted in any form or by any means, electronic, mechanical, photocopying, recording or otherwise, without the prior permission of the publisher. The name Usborne and the devices ⊕ ♀ are Trade Marks of Usborne Publishing Ltd. UE.